Jon's Bouncing Ball

Yellowstone National Park

Written by Marva Dale Bicknell

Illustrated by Artomel Black

GOLDMINDS

This book is dedicated to the Elders and Chieftains from innumerable indigenous tribes in the North, Central, and South American continents, who keep our traditions alive and teach us to follow the Red Road (right path).

We proclaim our heritage as native sons and daughters with pride and will keep Mother Earth sacred for many generations to come, to be loved and shared by all.

Marva Dale Bicknell

Jon's Bouncing Ball: Yellowstone National Park
Text by Marva Dale Bicknell
Art & design by Artomel Black
Text copyright © 2015 Marva Dale Bicknell
Illustration copyright © 2015 Goldminds Publishing
ISBN 978-1-942905-34-9
Library of Congress Control Number 2011928604

Goldminds Publishing, LLC
1050 Glenbrook Way, Suite 480
Hendersonville, TN 37075
www.goldmindspub.com

The illustrations in the book were created in watercolor and ink on paper.

To Yellowstone Park, I went on vacation
to see our national treasure of great admiration!

I bounced my ball, dribbling past the "Old Faithful Geyser,"
an ancient Arapaho elder said, "He will make you much wiser!"

I passed a mountain man panning for gold.
He hit a big lick and laughed out of control!

Then with a roaring voice I heard him scold,
"Do not tell anyone Yellowstone has riches of gold!"

I bounced my ball on to the warmth of Mammoth Hot Springs.
Looking up to the sky, I saw Mr. Raven spread his great wings.

High from the sky, I saw Mr. Raven swoop down.
He landed in a tree far off the ground.

He kept one eye on the horizon toward the distant sea, and the other he directly focused to guard and protect me.

With slingshot in hand, I ran down the riverbank.
I laughed as I slung it, "What an amusing prank!"

I skipped a few stones across the top of the water,
and to my enormous surprise, up popped an otter!

On Yellowstone River, I boarded a rugged ol' boat,
and then rested my head on a leisurely float.

I reached Gardner River Canyon in the middle of the day,
spread out a picnic lunch and had plans to stay.

Then up in the treetops I heard Mr. Raven ca
I followed his urgings up Mt. Evert's wall.

...a place that has stood for ten-thousand years, or more,
in the care of its people, the Arapaho.

They knew of its value, they knew of its worth,
it wasn't the gold; it was **"Mother Earth."**

"Care for the animals, water, and land,
and she will live on through many life spans."

I drew nearer to his presence as he continued to speak.

"If you neglect and misuse her, she will become weak."

"Mother Earth loves you, so return it in kind.
Care for her always and her love you will find."

Mr. Raven cawed, "Jon, it is time to return home.
Just know you and your ball will never be alone.

Mother Earth is under your feet, and I am watching with Father Sky."
That is what Mr. Raven said, as he stretched out his wings to fly.

References

Page 1. Yellowstone National Park was founded in 1872 and is considered to be one of the greatest U.S. National Treasures.

Page 3. Old Faithful Geyser erupts every 90 to 120 minutes and was named for the regularity of its eruptions.

Page 4. Throughout the Yellowstone region today, historic gold mining district hold festivals, and tourists are allowed to pan for gold. However, panning for gold and use of metal detectors is not allowed in Yellowstone National Park.

Page 7. Mammoth Hot Springs is a large complex of hot springs in Yellowstone National Park. It was created over thousands of years as hot water from the spring cooled and deposited calcium carbonate. Over two tons flow into Mammoth each day in a solution.

Page 10. The North American River Otter or more commonly called, "otter" is found in waterways and coastal regions on the North American Continent. They weigh between five and fourteen pounds and have a thick, water repellent coat.

Page 12. The Yellowstone River is a tributary of the Missouri River, in the Western United States.

Page 13. The Gardner River flows through Gardner Canyon, a heavily frequented tourist site and is also home to a popular hot spring known as, "The Boiling River."

Page 14. Mt. Everts is a peak near Mammoth Hot Springs in Yellowstone Park.

Page 16. The Yellowstone Park is in Montana and Idaho. The tribes of the First Nations (First Americans, Native Americans, Indigenous Peoples) living in Yellowstone prior to Euro-Americans were the Northern Arapaho, Eastern Shoshone, and Nez Perce.

Page 22. First Nation spiritual teachings refer to the earth as, "Mother," the sky as, "Father," and all things as interconnected, each depending upon the other(s) for survival.

"Return it in kind"

What do you do to care for the earth?

Do you plant trees and flowers?

Do you water and care for them?

Do you feed and take care of your animals?

Do you dispose of waste in its rightful place?

KEEP OUR WATER CLEAN!

CPSIA information can be obtained
at www.ICGtesting.com
Printed in the USA
LVOW05s0547251115
464077LV00013B/49/P